Ellie and the Butterfly Kitten

For Frances, Rachel, Richard,
Jordan, Danielle, Tom and Jenny
G.L.

For Emma
K.L.

ORCHARD BOOKS
96 Leonard Street, London EC2A 4XD
Orchard Books Australia
Unit 31/56 O'Riordan Street, Alexandria, NSW 2015
ISBN 1 84121 721 2 (hardback)
ISBN 1 84121 632 1 (paperback)
First published in Great Britain in 2000
First paperback publication in 2001
Text © Gillian Lobel 2000
Illustrations © Karin Littlewood 2000
The right of Gillian Lobel and Karin Littlewood to be identified as the author
and illustrator respectivelyof this work has been asserted by them
in accordance with the Copyright, Design and Patents Act, 1988.
A CIP catalogue record for this book is available from the British Library
1 2 3 4 5 6 7 8 9 10 (hardback)
1 2 3 4 5 6 7 8 9 10 (paperback)
Printed in Dubai

Ellie and the Butterfly Kitten

by Gillian Lobel

illustrated by Karin Littlewood

ORCHARD BOOKS

"Look what I found on the beach this morning," said Nanna.

It was a piece of blue glass, polished silky smooth by the sea.

"It's magic!" said Ellie.

Ellie loved staying at Nanna's house,
but this time it was without Mum.

Mum had been poorly,
and was going to hospital
for a while to be made better.
When they waved goodbye,
Ellie tried hard not to cry.

Nanna hugged her. "It won't be for long, sweetheart. Tomorrow we'll go treasure-hunting on the beach!"

Straight after breakfast Ellie ran down to the beach and splashed along the water's edge. It was a good day for treasure. She found a pearly shell and a coil of driftwood freckled with rusty gold and black.

Nanna and Ellie came to an old fishing
boat, pulled up high on the shore. Ellie
scrambled inside. It made a wonderful hideaway.
There in the shadows something gleamed – a curl
of wood, white, spangled with gold, and tiger stripes.
Ellie picked it up.

But it wasn't wood – it was soft and furry! It stirred faintly in her hands and opened bright blue eyes.

"Mew!" it cried. "Mew!"

"Oh, you poor baby!" Ellie held the soggy bundle close.

"Whatever have you got there!" said Nanna.

"A kitten, Nanna, a kitten!"

"It's a little girl," said Nanna, "and she's half frozen with cold. Tuck her in your jacket, Ellie. We'll take her straight home."

In the warmth of the kitchen Ellie rubbed the kitten's sodden little body with an old towel until her fur stood out like a dandelion clock.

Nanna made warm scrambled eggs.
The kitten sucked up the food hungrily.

Then Ellie lifted the kitten gently onto her lap,
and stroked her with one finger. She purred and purred.
"Oh, Nanna, look – she's got a little mark just like
a butterfly on her nose! Can we keep her – please?"
"Well…for the moment. But tomorrow we should
make enquiries – somebody must have lost her."
"Oh!" Suddenly Ellie felt sad.

The next day as soon as it was light, Ellie rushed downstairs. The kitten ran to meet her, her little tail standing straight up.

"I shall call you Butterfly," said Ellie, "because you've got a funny butterfly mark on your nose."

Nanna and Ellie made a notice about Butterfly for the local shop.

FOUND
Fluffy white kitten
flecked with gold and black.
About five weeks old.
Please telephone 0146 233458

And Ellie drew a beautiful picture of Butterfly in the corner. But she hoped so much that no one would claim her.

Ellie and Butterfly were always together.

Ellie fed her,

brushed her,

and played
with her,

and at night Butterfly snuggled up in bed with her.

Every evening Ellie spoke to Mum
on the phone to tell her what she and
Butterfly had been doing together.

Days went by and
no one phoned to claim Butterfly.
She's my kitten, thought Ellie. She's mine!

But then one day the telephone rang – and it wasn't Mum.
Ellie stopped playing with Butterfly to listen.

"Yes," Nanna was saying. "Yes – a butterfly mark on her
nose. Yes, and one ginger paw. Shall we bring her over
to you?" Nanna scribbled on a piece of paper.

Then she put her arm round Ellie.
"I'm afraid it sounds like Butterfly."

"Oh, no," said Ellie.

"I know, sweetheart…but we must take
Butterfly back – she's too young
to leave her mother."

They set off in the car. Ellie hugged the cat basket tightly all the way.

"Perhaps Butterfly's not their kitten," she said over and over again.

When they arrived, Nanna undid the basket and Butterfly ran towards a beautiful tortoiseshell cat. She licked the little kitten lovingly from head to tail.

Then Ellie watched as Butterfly snuggled up against her mother's warm fur.

And suddenly, more than anything in the world, Ellie wanted her own Mum.

"Let's go home, sweetheart," said Nanna.

Ellie was quiet all the way
to Nanna's. Then, as they reached the
house Ellie saw Mum's little car in the drive.
Her heart skipped a beat as she ran up the path.

Ellie whirled into the kitchen.
"Mum, oh, Mum!"
She buried her face in her mother's hair.
"Where's Butterfly then?" asked Mum.
"She was so little," said Ellie.
"She needed her own Mum…
just like me!"